To Siân, my baby sister
S. L.-J.

For my mum and her baby brother (Uncle George)
D. R.

Text copyright © 2017 by Sally Lloyd-Jones
Illustrations copyright © 2017 by David Roberts

First U.S. edition 2017

Library of Congress Catalog Card Number pending
ISBN 978-0-7636-9793-8

17 18 19 20 21 22 CCP 10 9 8 7 6 5 4 3 2 1

Printed in Shenzhen, Guangdong, China

This book was typeset in Avenir.
The illustrations were done in watercolor and pen.

Candlewick Press
99 Dover Street
Somerville, Massachusetts 02144

visit us at www.candlewick.com

CANDLEWICK PRESS

HIS ROYAL HIGHNESS, KING BABY

A Terrible True Story

Sally Lloyd-Jones

illustrated by

David Roberts

Once
upon a time,

there was a Happy Family:

a mom,

a dad,

a gerbil,

and the most beautifulest, cleverest, ever-so-kindest
Princess with long, flowing wondrous hair.
(In fact, actually, she is
ME!)

They all lived happily together in the Land, where there was always time for stories, plenty of room on your mom's lap, and absolutely NEVER any screaming.

Until one horrible, NOT NICE day, when a new ruler was born . . .

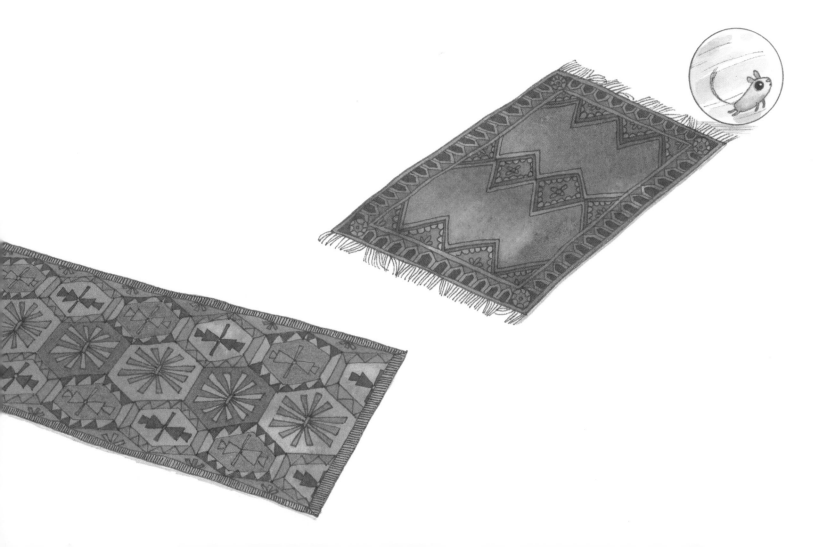

Behold~
His Royal Highness, King Baby!

No sooner had the baby arrived than suddenly
there was no talk in all the Land except:

"Such a nice big BURP!" and "Oh what a lovely POO-POO!"

completely NONSTOP ALL THE TIME!

It came to pass that the baby, instead of going away,
only grew fatter.

And even fatter still . . . He got a tooth . . . And a bit of hair . . .

And after A WHOLE ENTIRE YEAR of his Wicked Rule,
the Tragical Day arrived . . .

The King's First Birthday!

At the very stroke of 6:15 o'clock,
the darling Princess was woken by the rude
and very awful shouty shrieking of . . .

The Darling Birthday Boy!
Ruler of the Land!
His Royal Tinyness, King Baby!

The gentle girl (lovely in all her ways) had to cook her own breakfast—ALONE BY HERSELF— like a poor orphan child. But meanwhile . . .

BEHOLD His Royal Hungriness,
His Really Rather Greediness!
His Royal Roundness, King Baby!

After breakfast,
the cruelly mistreated
Princess hardly
even got a turn
in the bathroom.
But meanwhile . . .

BEHOLD His Royal
Clean-and-Sparkliness!
(What a Smelly!)
King Baby.

Then the kindhearted girl (as beautiful as a spring flower), clothed only in a raggedy old dress (that she had grown out of ages ago), was turned by her cruel almost-stepmother into a servant and had to tidy up her WHOLE ENTIRE bedroom with completely no help from anybody.

But meanwhile . . .

BEHOLD *Majesty Boy!*
(Such a sight to see!)
His Almost Perfectness, King Baby.

Next, the tender girl (of such delicate, dainty feet) was made to march all around the shops, carrying a bag that was SO ENORMOUS her arms almost fell off. And then she was forced to run BEHIND the Splendid Carriage—wherein rested the Royal Bottom . . .

BEHOLD! His One-and-Only Spoiledness, King Baby!

From Far and Wide, at last, the Royal Guests arrived.
His Lordships, Her Ladyships, Their Grandpa-and-Grandma-ships,
His Uncle-ships, Her Auntie-ships, and even Their Furry Pet-ships.

They came bearing gifts! Kneeling before him! Kissing his toes!
Speaking only in Nonsense! *"Bubba-Dubba-Wub!"* *"Ickle-Tickle-*
Pickle-Poo!" *"Wispsy-Wopsy-Woo!"*

The Whole Land was under an Enchantment!
She had become an invisible girl in her own home.
What could the poor innocent Princess do?

The Princess knew EXACTLY!

She would come to the party disguised as
a Mysterious Fairy,
with a magic wand,
a big very magical nose,
and a cunning plan . . .

It was time to break the spell!
She would tell all the Land
the terrible TRUE story!

The Mysterious Fairy took a deep breath . . .

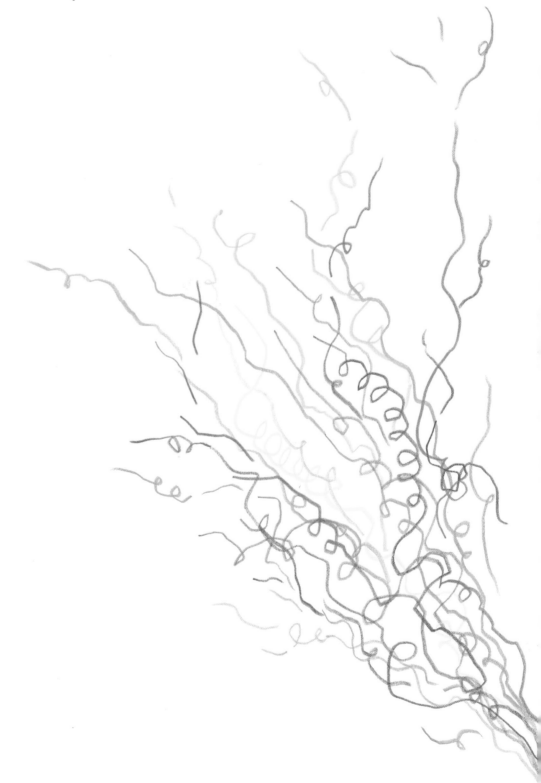

"Once upon a time . . ."

But before she could even begin,
there appeared a Giant Cake
of Chocolate with candles on top!
Everyone was singing!
The King was crowned:

Happy Birthday to HIM!
Happy Birthday to HIM!
Happy Birthday, Dear

(His Really Annoying Boringness)!
Happy Birthday to HIM!

Scarcely had these words been sung, when

HARK!

A Royal Scream echoed around the Palace.

BEHOLD

His Royal Unhappiness!
With Royal Drool all dribbling down!

WAAAAAAA-O-E-E-AAARGH!

His Lordships,
Her Ladyships,
Their Grandpa-and-Grandma-ships,
His Uncle-ships,
Her Auntie-ships,
and even Their Furry Pet-ships swooped,
and dabbed, and wiped, and mopped.

"Oh, dear!" they cried.
"Who didn't have their nap?"
"Off to bed!"
"Say night-night!"
"Wave bye-bye!"

His poor Birthday Highness only screamed louder.

And even LOUDER still . . .

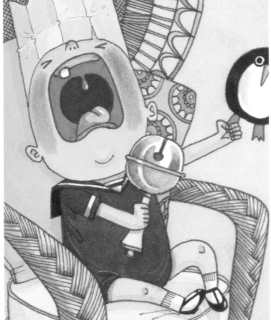

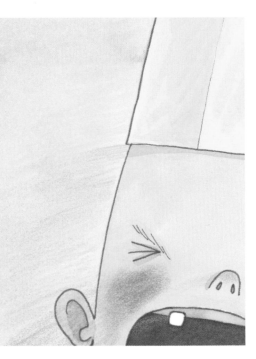

He kicked his legs!

He thumped his fists!

He shook his head!

He threw down . . .

 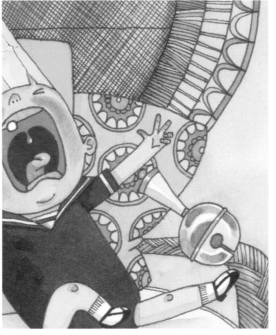 

his Orb!   his Scepter!   his Royal Crown!

Despite all that had befallen her, the Kind Fairy's loveliness had grown ever stronger (like a sparkling mountain stream). She would rescue him! "Don't cry, Mr. Baby," she whispered in his ear.

And she kissed his cheek.

IN AN INSTANT, his screaming was cured!

He smiled, and giggled, and pointed at her ugly nose.

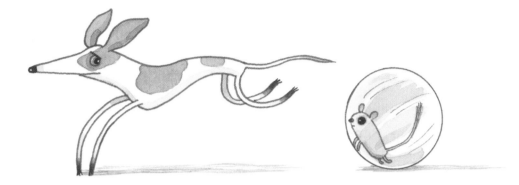

"My Brother and I must do our Coloring NOW!" the Fairy declared to All the Land. "We are leaving WITHOUT DELAY!"

And so they did. Together. Holding hands.

But not before the little King issued a Royal Decree:

"Blupp dob Bip? Op nopp!"

(Which is Baby for "BEHOLD!
My Favorite and My Best Princess Big Sister
EVER in the whole WORLD!")
(Basically.)

And the end of the story is

They Lived Happily Ever After—

THE END . . .

a mom,

a dad,

a gerbil,

a brother,

and the most beautifulest, cleverest, ever-so-kindest
Princess Big Sister, with long, flowing wondrous hair.

(PS: The King was too little to eat his birthday cake, so, out of
the goodness of her heart, the Princess ate his piece for him.)